SWEETAPPLE FARM

WENDY SMITH

HUTCHINSON
LONDON SYDNEY AUCKLAND JOHANNESBURG

The sun comes up   as the moon goes down.

The cock crows,

'COCK-A-DOODLE-DOO!'

The day is starting at Sweetapple Farm.

Cows moo.   Horses neigh.   Ducks quack.

Geese honk.   Pigs grunt.

Sheep bleat.

The farm dog barks.

Chickens cluck.

The farm cat mews.

The alarm clock rings at
Sweetapple Farm,

BOING! BOING! BOING!

The farmer yawns. The farmer's wife yawns. The baby yells.

Little Jack gets up and cleans his teeth.

Granny gets up and cleans her teeth.

The cat gets up and cleans her kittens.

And everyone screams,

'WHERE'S MY

oink

cluck

wuff

BREAKFAST?'

quack quack quack

pop
pop
pop

tap
tap

slop
slop

Mrs Brown feeds Jack, Granny and Ann, the baby.

Jack feeds his rabbit.

Granny feeds her budgie.

Mr Brown feeds the cockerel

and the hens.

He waters the horses.

And milks the cows.

He gathers some eggs.

And tethers the goats.

He shepherds his sheep.

And looks down on his farm.

'GOOD MORNING!'

Mr Brown says as he comes in for his breakfast.

Jack goes to school.

Granny goes to market.

Mrs Brown goes to plough.

She grows

barley,   corn   and peas.

Mr Brown makes hay.

While

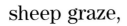

sheep graze,

cattle low,

horses trot,

pigs snuffle,

birds tweet.

Jack comes home.   Granny comes home.

The sun sinks low on Sweetapple Farm.

And everyone
has their
supper.

chomp
chomp

chew
chew

munch munch

mmm!

Mrs Brown baths the baby.

Mr Brown puts her to bed.

Jack plays with the cat.

Roses are red love
and violets
are blue ...

Granny plays the mouth organ.

Silence
is golden

Mrs Brown plays the piano.

Mr Brown plays the fool.

The moon comes up.

The animals lie down.

Jack goes to bed.

Granny goes to sleep.

BONG! BONG! BONG! BONG!

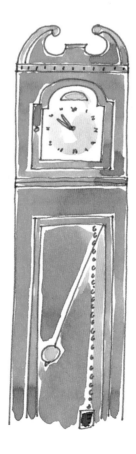

chimes the grandfather clock.

'GOOD NIGHT!'

says Mr Brown and Mrs Brown and Granny as they go up to bed.

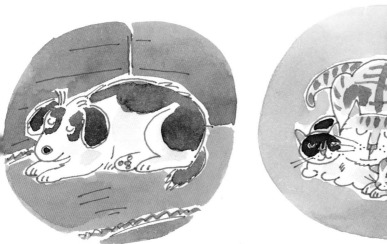  

Now everyone sleeps.

The moon shines brightly.

Stars are twinkling.

The barn owl hoots,

'TU-WHIT, TU-WHOO!'

The day has ended on Sweetapple Farm.